This book belongs to:

♦ ♦ ♦ ♦ ♦ ♦ ♦ ♦ ♦ ♦ ♦ ♦ ♦

For Sue and Anil,
upon whose idea this book is based

Also by Sarah Garson:
DAYDREAM DAN

First published in Great Britain in 2009 by Andersen Press Ltd.,
20 Vauxhall Bridge Road, London SW1V 2SA.
Published in Australia by Random House Australia Pty.,
Level 3, 100 Pacific Highway, North Sydney, NSW 2060.
Copyright © Sarah Garson, 2009.
The rights of Sarah Garson to be identified as the author and illustrator of this work
have been asserted by her in accordance with the Copyright, Designs and Patents Act, 1988.
All rights reserved.
Colour separated in Switzerland by Photolitho AG, Zürich.
Printed and bound in Singapore.

10   9   8   7   6   5   4   3   2   1

British Library Cataloguing in Publication Data available.

ISBN 978 1 84270 722 7 (hardback)
ISBN 978 1 84270 947 4 (paperback)

This book has been printed on acid-free paper

The GRUMP

Sarah Garson

Andersen Press

Early one morning . . .

. . . . a scary monster crept into my bedroom . . . .

sneaked along the landing . . .

. . . and disappeared from sight.

It had made a dreadful
mess in the bathroom . . .

. . . and left a trail of gigantic footprints all the way down the stairs.

Then it padded into the kitchen . . .

. . . and gobbled up
everything in sight!

Something loomed
at the door . . . .

Phew! It was only Mum
and my baby brother.

They had heard the
monster too.

We followed the
sound of deep, rumbling
growls . . .

It was him!

THE GRUMP!

My very own grumpy,
sleepy dad . . .

. . . and not a scary
monster at all!

Also by Sarah Garson:

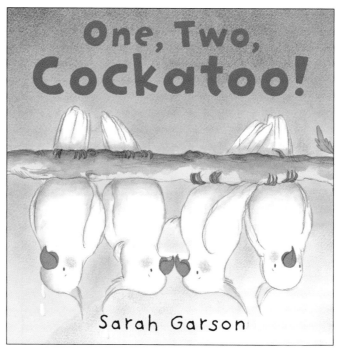